Maryam
the Nurse
Fairy

Join the **Rainbow Magic Reading Challenge!**

Read the story and collect your fairy points to climb the

~~Reading Rainbow at the back of the book!~~

To Tamsyn, who is brave and kind

Special thanks to
Rachel Elliot

ORCHARD BOOKS

First published in Great Britain in 2021 by The Watts Publishing Group

1 3 5 7 9 10 8 6 4 2

© 2021 Rainbow Magic Limited.
© 2021 HIT Entertainment Limited.
Illustrations © 2021 The Watts Publishing Group Limited.

A CIP catalogue record for this book is available from the British Library.

ISBN 978 1 40836 466 6

Printed and bound in Great Britain by Clays Ltd, Elcograf S.p.A

MIX
Paper from
responsible sources
FSC® C104740

The paper and board used in this book are made from wood from responsible sources

Orchard Books
An imprint of Hachette Children's Group
Part of The Watts Publishing Group Limited
Carmelite House, 50 Victoria Embankment, London EC4Y 0DZ

An Hachette UK Company
www.hachette.co.uk
www.hachettechildrens.co.uk

Maryam
the Nurse
Fairy

By Daisy Meadows

ORCHARD

www.orchardseriesbooks.co.uk

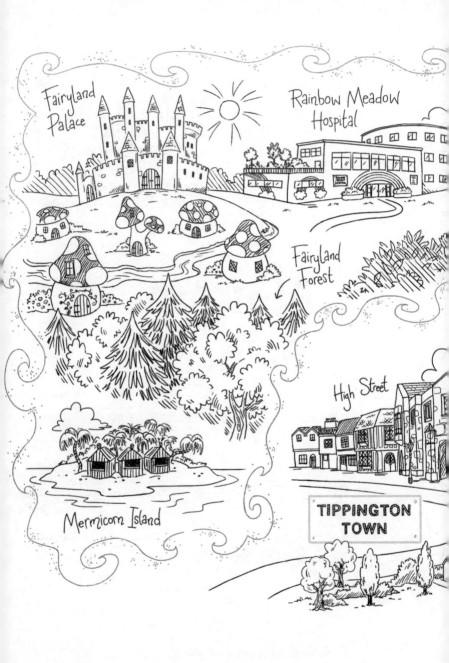

Fairyland Palace

Rainbow Meadow Hospital

Fairyland Forest

High Street

Mermicorn Island

TIPPINGTON TOWN

Jack Frost's Spell

A human or a fairy nurse –
I can't decide which one is worse!
But with the fob watch in my hand,
They'll suffer under my command.

Nurses will be filled with greed,
Forget to comfort those in need.
A brand-new era will begin –
And spitefulness will always win!

Contents

Chapter One
Visiting Margot

"Which is your cousin's favourite flavour?" said Kirsty Tate.

She gazed at the colourful rows of ice cream tubs in the hospital shop freezer. Her best friend, Rachel Walker, pointed to a tub of Marshmallow Chocolate Biscuit Crunch.

"That's the one that Margot likes best," she said.

Rachel's cousin Margot was in City Hospital for a simple operation. Her tonsils had been taken out, and she had to eat soft, easy food for a few days. Rachel took some money out of her kitten-shaped purse and paid for the ice cream.

"Come on, you two," said Mr Walker from the shop doorway. "It's visiting time."

Mr and Mrs Walker led the way to the colourful children's department. It was bustling with busy, smiling nurses, and the nurses' station was decorated with hearts and stars.

"Hi, we're here to see Margot," said Mrs Walker.

"She's in Rainbow Ward," said a young nurse, smiling. "You've chosen a great day for a visit. We have a magician coming in later. I'm Josh, by the way."

He led them to a bay where the walls and windows were covered with paintings of rainbows. Rachel and Kirsty shared a quick smile. For them, rainbows had a secret meaning. The first fairies they ever met had looked after the colours of the rainbow. Since then, the girls had been to Fairyland many times, and had helped lots of fairies. But rainbows still held a special place in their hearts.

Margot was sitting up in bed, and her mother was on the chair beside her.

"Hi, Aunt Willow," Rachel called out. "Hi, Margot, how are you feeling?"

Margot smiled and waved her hand.

Aunt Willow jumped up and hugged them all.

"It's great to see you all," she said. "I'm glad you're here too, Kirsty. I haven't seen you since we found the Lost City."

Aunt Willow was a famous explorer, and the girls had been lucky enough

to join her on an expedition to the
Congo. They had even shared a magical
adventure with Ellen the Explorer Fairy
at the same time.

"How's my lovely niece?" asked Mr
Walker, bending over to give Margot a
hug.

"She's doing well," said Aunt Willow.
"But she has rather a sore throat."

"We've got just the thing," said Rachel,
showing Margot the ice cream. "Your
favourite! Shall we go and find a bowl
and a spoon?"

Margot's eyes sparkled.

"Yes please," she whispered, nodding
eagerly.

Rachel and Kirsty went back to the
nurses' station. Josh was there, but his big
smile had faded. The other nurses were

looking more serious too.

"Hi, Josh," said Kirsty. "Please could we have a bowl and a spoon for some ice cream?"

"Of course," said Josh. "Just a minute."

He tapped the computer keyboard and looked at another nurse with a worried frown.

"It's definitely gone," he said.

"The whole day's timetable is lost," said the second nurse, groaning. "Now we don't know who is meant to be working when or where. How could the computer have deleted the file?"

"I'm sorry to bother you at a time like this," said Rachel. "If we could have a bowl and a spoon then we will get out of the way."

Josh's eyes widened.

"Oh no," he exclaimed, staring at the
screen. "The list of medicines has been
jumbled up."

"I can't find out which nurse is
supposed to be caring for which patient,"
said the second nurse, checking another
computer. "All the files have vanished."

Rachel and Kirsty felt sorry for them.

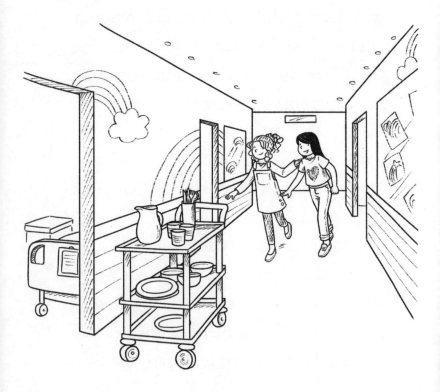

"Let's try to find a bowl ourselves," said Kirsty. "It sounds as if the nurses are going to be busy for a while."

Around another corner, they found a little trolley filled with plates, cutlery, jugs, cups and bowls.

"Perfect," said Rachel, picking up a little bowl and a spoon. "Ice cream, here we come."

She turned to go back to the ward, but Kirsty didn't move. She was staring at a glass jug on top of the trolley. It was glimmering with rainbow colours and seemed to be filled with blue mist. The girls knew at once that there was only one explanation. Magic!

Chapter Two
Rainbow Meadow Hospital

Suddenly, blue mist spiralled out of the jug. A tiny fairy was standing on tiptoe on the highest peak of the mist. She was wearing light-blue scrubs decorated with rainbows and clouds, and her long, dark hair gleamed in the bright hospital lights.

"I'm Maryam the Nurse Fairy," she

said. "I'm glad to meet you, Rachel and
Kirsty."

"It's lovely to meet you too," said
Rachel. "Are you
here to look after
the children's
nurses? We saw
that they were
having a hard time
just now."

"I'm afraid
that things are
only going to
get worse," said
Maryam. "Will you
come to Fairyland
with me? Queen
Titania herself sent
me to find you."

"What's wrong?" Kirsty asked.

"Today, there was a special ceremony in Fairyland," said Maryam. "Queen Titania opened our brand-new Rainbow Meadow Hospital. But thanks to Jack Frost, my precious magical fob watch has been stolen. It helps me to look after children's nurses in Fairyland and all over the human world. I make sure that they have enough time, love and energy to do their job. Without it, I can't help them."

Rachel glanced back around the corner. The nurses were still staring at the computer screen. No one was watching the girls.

"Time for a visit to Fairyland!" she said.

The girls knew that fairy magic would return them to the human world as if no time had passed. Maryam sprinkled them with a flurry of tiny, glittering rainbows, and they shrank to fairy size. Pearly wings appeared on their shoulders. Then blue mist swirled around them and they felt themselves whizzing away from the human world.

When the mist cleared, they were hovering over a building in a Fairyland meadow. It was the colour of the summer sky, with rainbows and clouds painted on the walls.

"Welcome to the Rainbow Meadow Hospital," said Maryam.

She proudly led Rachel and Kirsty through the glass entrance doors. The first thing they saw was a rainbow-shaped nurses' station. Two of the Helping Fairies – Perrie the Paramedic Fairy and

Martha the Doctor Fairy – were standing there with Queen Titania, while fairy nurses fluttered in and out of the wards. Crowds of fairy guests were milling around the waiting area, talking in low, worried voices.

The queen looked extremely relieved to see Rachel and Kirsty.

"Once again, we must call upon your help, girls," she said, smiling.

Rachel and Kirsty curtseyed.

"We'll do whatever we can, Your Majesty," said Kirsty.

"I hope that you can help Maryam," said Queen Titania. "She is a brave, strong and caring nurse."

"Nurses choose to do a job that puts others first," said Martha. "That makes them very special."

"We can't allow Jack Frost to put their work in danger," Perrie added.

There was a tinkling sound, and everyone whirled around.

"Sorry," said a fairy nurse, who had dropped a shining needle threaded with spider silk.

"I remember Saffron the Yellow Fairy

mending Queenie's wings with one of those," said Rachel.

A second fairy nurse paused by the nurses' station.

"I've forgotten which bed my patient is in," she said, blushing.

Just then, a third fairy nurse walked past, tapping a little bottle with her wand. With every tap, the liquid inside changed colour. Red. Purple. Gold. Silver.

"I know this spell inside out," she was muttering. "I cure the Barn Elf's cold every year. Why can't I remember it?"

"How has this happened?" asked Rachel.

"I will show you," said Queen Titania.

She blew a little fairy dust against the wall behind the nurses' station. It shimmered and then transformed into a glimmering film screen.

"It's just like the Seeing Pool," Kirsty whispered.

On the film screen, they saw a crowd of smiling fairies in the waiting area, including Maryam, Martha and Perrie. Kirsty gasped when she saw Jack Frost there, scowling with his arms folded. Queen Titania cut a ribbon and declared the hospital open, and everyone clapped and cheered.

Suddenly, Jack Frost jumped to his feet. A cold, grey mist began to swirl around his feet.

"This is boring," he said in a loud, chilly voice. "Why is everyone praising these silly nurse fairies? No one ever praises me!"

He clicked his fingers and the grey mist spread further. Then there was a commotion at the back of the crowd. Fairies cried out as three goblins elbowed them aside. Each one had a coloured bandana around his neck – one lime green, one yellow and one rust orange.

"Now things will get interesting," said Jack Frost, cackling. "Say hello to my naughtiest goblins!"

Chapter Three
Three Naughty Goblins

The three goblins swaggered up to the nurses' station. Rachel and Kirsty held their breath as they watched.

"I need a nurse," said the one with the lime-green bandana. "I've sprained my belly button."

"I want some medicine," shouted the

yellow goblin. "I've twisted my armpit."

"Nurse, nurse, my bottom is broken," the rust-orange goblin exclaimed. "Bring out your ointment!"

He snatched Maryam's stethoscope and waved it around his head like a lasso.

"Why did the doctor lose his temper?" he yelled.

"Because he didn't have any patients," squawked the goblin with the lime-green bandana.

The three goblins fell to the floor and rolled around, cackling and clutching their stomachs. Jack Frost's spiky beard quivered as he laughed. Queen Titania stepped forwards.

"Stop this at once," she said, "or I will send these naughty goblins back to where they came from."

"But my naughty goblins came from so many different places," said Jack Frost in a mocking, sing-song voice. "Teasing mermicorns at sea, pestering humans, irritating shy forest creatures – their work is never done."

He rubbed his bony hands together in

chilly glee.

"I want one of those uniforms," whined the goblin with the yellow bandana, snatching at the scrubs of a nearby nurse fairy.

"Give me that," said the goblin wearing the lime-green bandana, grabbing a tray out of her hands.

Cotton wool balls flew into the air.

"It's snowing!" he yelled, flinging the balls around.

The goblin with the rust-orange bandana pulled a bandage out of another nurse fairy's pocket. He raced through the waiting area, wrapping the bandage around the fairy crowd.

"Spingle spangle, fairies in a tangle," he sang out.

Jack Frost leaned back, holding his sides

as he laughed helplessly. Queen Titania
pointed her wand at the three goblins.

"By order of the Fairy Queen, return at
once to where
you've been."

POP!
The goblins
disappeared.
Maryam looked
down to check
the time, and
gasped.

"Oh no, my
fob watch," she
said. "They've
taken it."

"A lot of
things are
missing,"

said another nurse fairy. "Plasters, thermometers, bandages . . ."

Maryam ran to the nurses' station.

"My list has gone too," she said with a groan.

"Your list?" asked the queen.

"I keep a list of all the nurses in the human world," Maryam explained. "Once a year, I give every nurse a treat to say thank you. It's always something small, like a bunch of flowers or a yummy cake. But without the list and the

watch, I can't deliver the treats."

"How interesting," hissed Jack Frost.

His eyes glittered like an icy morning, and Maryam looked horrified.

"I forgot he was here," she said.

With a cackle of triumph, and a flash of blue lightning, Jack Frost vanished. The picture on the wall faded, and Maryam turned to Rachel and Kirsty.

"Now he knows about my special fob watch, he's gone to find the goblin who took it," she said. "But how can we find out which goblin it was? And how can we get there first?"

"Jack Frost told us where the goblins came from," said Rachel. "He mentioned mermicorns in the sea, shy creatures in the forest, and the human world."

"But that doesn't tell us exactly where

to look," said Maryam.

"Maybe it does," said Kirsty slowly. "We met mermicorns during our adventure with Evelyn the Mermicorn Fairy, and we went to a faraway forest with Robyn the Christmas Party Fairy. Perhaps they can help us."

"We're here!" called a voice like a silver bell.

"That's Evelyn!" Kirsty exclaimed.

Evelyn and Robyn came flying out of the crowd in the waiting area.

"We heard everything," said Robyn, straightening the thin golden band in her hair. "If we touch our wands to Maryam's wand, I can give you the directions to the forest where the Barn Elf lives, and Evelyn can tell you where the mermicorns are at this time of year."

They pressed the tips of their wands to Maryam's wand, and there was a fizz of magical sparkles.

"Good luck," said Robyn.

"And don't forget to give the mermicorns my love," added Evelyn.

Rachel, Kirsty and Maryam ran out of the Rainbow Meadow Hospital. Maryam pointed her wand into the air, and a shining trail of gemstones appeared.

"Follow those jewels!" said Rachel.

Chapter Four
On the Trail

Soon, the three fairies were zooming out to sea. The jewel trail led them over the sparkling waves, around Festival Island, and then curved downwards. A small speedboat was chasing three mermicorns, and the goblin with the yellow bandana was at the wheel.

Rachel, Kirsty and Maryam dived downwards and landed in a heap in the back of the boat. The goblin squealed in shock and tumbled over backwards. With the wheel spinning, the speedboat went wildly out of control.

"The key!" Rachel shouted.

Maryam lunged forwards and turned the key. The engine stopped and the boat slowed down. The three mermicorns – Topaz, Garnet and Emerald – flicked

their tails and shook their manes in thanks.

"Evelyn sends her love," called Kirsty as the mermicorns swam away.

"You pesky, interfering insects," the goblin squawked. "You spoiled my fun!"

"It isn't fun to chase animals and scare them," said Kirsty in a firm voice.

Rachel was looking around the bottom of the boat. It was a mess of cotton wool and bandages.

"No fob watch, and no list," she said. "It wasn't this goblin who took them."

"Next stop, the forest," said Maryam.

Maryam pointed her wand into the air again, and a trail of golden stars appeared, curving back towards the land. The fairies rose into the air, with the goblin shaking his fist after them.

Maryam

It didn't take long to reach the dark-green forest where the Barn Elf lived. Almost at once, they heard loud shouts and saw bright flashes of light from below.

"Robyn said that the forest was full of shy creatures," said Kirsty. "Who could be making such a commotion?"

"Let's find out," said Maryam in a determined voice.

She dived down and disappeared into the canopy of trees. Rachel and Kirsty followed her. Even though the sun was bright, it couldn't pass through the thick leaves and tightly packed trees. It went dark so suddenly that the fairies felt as if they had plunged into night. They paused in a small clearing, trying to get used to the dim light.

"Oi, big ears!" cried a shrill voice.

A silvery hare broke out of the undergrowth and raced across the clearing.

"That's a moon hare," said Maryam with a gasp. "Goodness, I've never seen one in real life before. They are incredibly shy."

The moon hare was followed a second later by the goblin with the lime-green bandana. He was holding up a camera and snapping picture after picture. The

flash was blinding.

"Just a few photos," he squawked, cackling with laughter. "Come back here!"

The fairies darted in front of the goblin, who squealed, threw his camera into the air and promptly fell over. The camera landed in his hands and the flash went off in his face. He dropped his camera bag, and the contents spilled out on to the forest floor.

"OW!" he screeched, standing up. "That's too bright."

"It was too

bright for the poor moon hare too," said Kirsty. "How could you scare it like that?"

"It's just a silly animal," the goblin snapped.

"It's a living creature with feelings, just like you," said Rachel.

The goblin couldn't think of anything to say, so he stuck out his tongue at her. He started to pick up the things he had dropped. There were boxes of plasters and tubes of antiseptic cream, but no sign of the fob watch or the list. Kirsty raised her eyebrows.

"The goblin who went to the human world must be the one who took your things," she said to Maryam.

"But the human world is huge," said Rachel. "How can we possibly know where to look?"

"I don't know where to start looking," said Maryam. "But I can't stop thinking about the human nurses. Without my fob watch, their job will be even more challenging."

"Let's go back to the hospital where you found us," Kirsty suggested. "You can check on the nurses there and it will give us time to think of a plan."

"Great idea," said Maryam.

She waved her wand over their heads, and glittering fairy dust floated all around them. Moments later, they were back in City Hospital, at the end of the corridor where their adventure had begun.

"We're human again," said Rachel. "Goodness, that was so fast that I didn't even notice myself growing bigger."

Maryam tucked herself into Kirsty's T-shirt pocket.

"Please could we go to the nurses' station?" she asked. "I'm longing to know how they are coping."

It was hard to see the nurses' station because there were so many visitors standing around it, and all of them were talking at once. Some of them were shouting and waving their arms around.

"It's chaos," said Maryam with a groan. "The poor nurses!"

Chapter Five
Vanishing Act

The girls saw Josh talking to the crowd.

"Ladies and gentlemen, please be understanding," he was saying. "We are trying to find out the patient's bed numbers so that you can visit them. It's just that the list seems to have vanished."

In the middle of the crowd there was a

tall woman with a large trunk. She was wearing a flowing cape decorated with stars and moons.

"I'm here to do the magic show," she said in a loud, ringing voice. "Where shall I set up my equipment?"

Josh stared at her in alarm.

"But . . . but . . . you're two hours early," he stammered.

"Actually, I'm right on time," said the magician. "I did tell you when I would be arriving."

"I'm sorry," said Josh. "My watch must have stopped. Everything seems to be going wrong today."

A brown-haired nurse patted Josh on the back.

"I'll go and make all the visitors a pot of tea and then we can work out which beds their friends and relatives are in," she said. "You're doing a great job."

"That's one of the things I love about nursing," said Maryam. "The team cares for each other as well as for their patients."

The brown-haired nurse went into the staff room. Then the girls heard her cry out in surprise. They ran to the doorway and gasped.

"What a mess," said Kirsty.

There were empty biscuit wrappers all over the floor. Pictures were hanging crookedly on the walls, and the teapot and teacups had all been smashed. A bottle of milk had spilled across the carpet.

"This is goblins' work," Kirsty murmured, and then she felt a rush of hope. "Could the goblin with the rust-orange bandana be here?"

"Let's start looking," said Rachel. "If he's here in City Hospital, we'll find him."

They had just started searching an unused examination room when they heard a rumbling sound coming their way. *CRASH!* The doors burst open and the goblin with the rust-orange bandana shot through on a food trolley.

"WHEEEE!" he squealed.

The trolley rocketed past the girls and smashed against the wall. The goblin fell off, cackling with laughter.

"Best ride ever!" he yelled, jumping up.

"Look at his neck," Maryam exclaimed.

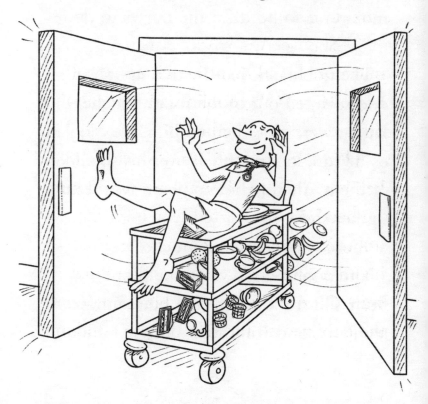

A small, silver fob watch was shining on the rust-orange bandana. Rachel held out her hands and took a step forward.

"We only want to talk to you," she said in a gentle voice.

"Not interested," said the goblin.

"Please listen," said Kirsty. "You're making it so hard for the nurses to do their job."

The goblin shoved the trolley at them and sprinted out of the room. Rachel and Kirsty were close behind him. He giggled as he ran, looking back over his shoulder at them. Ahead, the magician was setting up her show.

"Look out!" shouted Rachel.

The goblin skidded on the slippery floor, slid straight into the open magic trunk . . . and vanished.

"Goodness, what was that?" asked the magician, spinning around.

Luckily, a crowd of patients came around the corner at that moment, and she forgot about her question.

"Welcome, welcome all," she boomed. "As you find your seats, I will perform a few small spells."

Rachel waved to her parents, Aunt Willow and Margot.

"Abracadabra!" declared the magician.

A bunch of flowers popped from her sleeve.

"Alakazam!" She drew a string of coloured handkerchiefs from her mouth.

"Hocus pocus!" She pulled a goblin out of her hat.

"OW!" yelled the goblin. "Let go of my ears!"

Astonished, the magician let go and the goblin scampered off. The audience roared with laughter and clapped, thinking it was part of the show. The magician rubbed her forehead. She was having a very confusing time.

Kirsty grabbed Rachel's hand and chased the goblin down the corridor. He dodged sideways into a room and the girls followed him. It was dimly lit with coloured bubble tubes and glowing fairy lights.

"Ugh, what is that stink?" the goblin said in a disgusted voice.

"It's lavender," said Maryam. "It's a beautiful, calming smell. This is a sensory room. It's designed to calm patients down if they feel upset."

"It's horrible," squawked the goblin, scrunching up his nose. "Let me out."

"We just want to talk to you about the fob watch," said Rachel.

She closed the door and put her back against it.

"Please think about the poorly children on this ward," she said. "That fob watch you stole helps the nurses to look after them. But while you have it, the nurses will struggle to do their job."

"Stop burbling on about watches," the goblin wailed. "Turn on the lights!"

"Oh, the poor thing is scared of the dark," Kirsty realised.

She felt along the wall and turned the dimmer switch. Then she heard Rachel gasp, and whirled around.

Jack Frost was standing in the middle of the room!

Chapter Six
The Queen's Spell

"What a treat to see you again," Jack Frost sneered at the girls. "You're just in time to see me triumph."

He snatched the fob watch from the goblin, and a sheet of paper dropped from inside his bandana.

"My list," Maryam whispered.

"Victory,"
hissed Jack Frost,
clutching the
watch and the
list. "For once, I
WIN!"

There was a
sudden flash of
blue lightning,
and then a
dense mist
folded around
them.

"Oh, it's like
walking into a
freezer," said Rachel, shuddering.

The mist cleared, and the girls found
themselves standing beside Maryam
on the roof of the Rainbow Meadow

Hospital. Kirsty and Rachel reached out for each other. It felt strange to be fairy-sized but without wings.

"Why have you brought us back here?" asked Maryam.

"I want every fairy in Fairyland to see you fail," he replied, stamping loudly on the roof. "Come out, come out, wherever you are!"

Seconds later, a crowd of fairies emerged from the hospital. They gazed up at Jack Frost, looking shocked and worried. Queen Titania was among them.

"I like winning," said Jack Frost. "But seeing fairies lose is even better!"

He held the sheet of paper above his head, and the icy wind grew stronger. The rust-orange goblin sat at his feet and sniggered.

"Please give me back my things," Maryam said. "What use are they to you?"

"Good point," said Jack Frost, with a hard smile. "They're no use at all!"

He ripped up the paper and flung the tiny pieces into the wind.

"NO!" cried Rachel and Kirsty, as the

breeze carried the scraps of paper in all directions.

Jack Frost had stopped laughing. He was holding his hand and whimpering.

"Ow," he said in a surprised voice. "OW! My finger hurts."

"What is it?" asked Maryam.

"It's a paper cut," said Jack Frost in a horrified voice.

He sank to his knees, clutching his hand. The fob watch fell to the ground with a clonk, and Maryam rushed forward. She stepped over the fob watch and kneeled down beside Jack Frost, pulling a miniature first-aid kit from her scrubs pocket.

"There, there," she said. "Paper cuts are very sore. I'll make it better."

"It hurts," Jack Frost whimpered.

"I know," said Maryam in a soothing voice. "You are being very brave."

She rubbed a little cream on to his finger and then covered the cut with a plaster. Rachel stepped forward and picked up the fob watch. She pinned it on to Maryam's scrubs.

"I'm sorry about your list," she said.

"Oh my goodness," said Kirsty. "Look!"

Every single fairy, including the queen, was speeding across the meadow. Countless fairies tumbled, dived and swooped as the tiny scraps of paper danced on the wind.

"What are they doing?" asked Maryam in wonder.

Kirsty smiled. "Don't you know?" she asked.

One by one, the fairies returned, each holding a piece of the precious list. The Nurse Fairy's eyes sparkled with happy tears, and Rachel and Kirsty felt tears prickling their eyes too.

There was a shimmer of purple and gold, and Queen Titania appeared beside them. She handed the final scrap of paper to Maryam.

"Everyone here knows how important your work is," she said. "We want to help you honour all the nurses on this list."

"Claptrap, tommyrot and twaddle," said Jack Frost, jumping up with a scowl. "*I'm* the important one.

One day you fairies will realise that!"

He and the goblin vanished in a bright flash of lightning.

"And now, let's put things right," said the queen with a little smile.

She pressed the tip of her wand against the scrap of paper in Maryam's hand. A single strand of golden thread travelled from fairy to fairy, magically sewing the paper scraps back together. At last, the list was whole again. It fluttered into the air, and then landed softly in Maryam's hand.

"I'm speechless, Your Majesty," she said, curtseying. "Thank you. And thank *you*, Rachel and Kirsty. Without you, I wouldn't have known where to start looking."

"The king and I wish to thank you too," said Queen Titania, turning to Rachel and Kirsty. "Once again, you

have been there when we needed you."

"We're just glad that nurses will have Maryam's magical help again," said Kirsty.

The crowd of fairies around them burst into cheers and applause.

"I think it's time for us to go back to City Hospital," said Rachel. "After all, we have some ice cream to deliver."

Maryam hugged them both.

"What an adventure we've had," she whispered, smiling. "I'll never forget it."

She lifted her wand, and Rainbow Meadow flickered and blurred. The girls blinked, and they were back in City Hospital, just around the corner from the magic show.

"Ooh, my hands are freezing," said Rachel with a shiver.

She looked down and burst into laughter. She was holding a large bowl of ice cream in each hand. Kirsty had a bowl too.

"Marshmallow Chocolate Biscuit Crunch for Margot, and rainbow flavour for us," Kirsty said in delight.

"Come on, let's go and watch the magic show,' said Rachel, beaming. "I think this is the yummiest end to a fairy adventure yet!"

The End

**Now it's time for Kirsty and
Rachel to help ...**

Elisha the Eid Fairy

Read on for a sneak peek ...

The crescent moon was half hidden
behind wispy clouds, the midnight sky
glimmered with stars, and Rachel Walker
lay asleep in her bed. She was dreaming
of her many magical adventures in
Fairyland. Most people can only dream
of such a thing. But Rachel had often
visited Fairyland in real life. Only
her best friend, Kirsty Tate, shared the
wonderful secret that they were friends
with the fairies.

"Rachel!"

The loud whisper broke into Rachel's
dreams. Her eyelids flickered.

"Rachel!" came the whisper again.

Rachel frowned and opened her eyes. It sounded like Kirsty. But how *could* it be? Kirsty was miles away at home in Wetherbury.

"I must have dreamt it," Rachel murmured, closing her eyes and sinking back into sleep.

"Rachel!"

The voice was louder, and this time Rachel felt sure that she hadn't imagined it. She sat up and stared around the room. Who was speaking to her? She crossed her fingers. Please, *please* let this be the start of a new adventure!

"Hello?" she said.

There was an answering patter on the windowpane, like tiny drops of rain. Rachel jumped out of bed, her heart thudding with excitement. She ran to the window and flung open the curtains. Moonlight spilled into the room, and Rachel gasped. Kirsty was outside, fairy-sized, fluttering her gauzy wings against the glass.

Rachel's fingers trembled eagerly as she turned the handle and opened the window. Kirsty slipped inside.

"Brrr, it's cold out there," Kirsty said, rubbing her arms.

She was wearing pyjamas and a dressing gown. Rachel pinched herself to check that she wasn't still dreaming.

"How did you get here?" she asked. "And why are you fairy-sized? What's happened?"

Kirsty flew to Rachel's bed and snuggled under the corner of her blanket.

"I was asleep until about ten minutes ago," she said. "Then I felt something tugging on my earlobe. It was Elisha the Eid Fairy."

"Of course," said Rachel breathlessly. "The new moon is in the sky. Eid starts tonight!"

Read Elisha the Eid Fairy to find out what adventures are in store for Kirsty and Rachel!

Calling all parents, carers and teachers!
The Rainbow Magic fairies are here to help
your child enter the magical world of reading.
Whatever reading stage they are at, there's
a Rainbow Magic book for everyone!
Here is Lydia the Reading Fairy's guide to
supporting your child's journey at all levels.